DISCARD

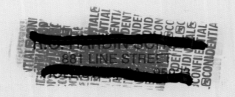

The Boy Who Lost His Belly Button

Jeanne Willis   Tony Ross

DK
Ink

DORLING KINDERSLEY
PUBLISHING, INC.

Dorling Kindersley Publishing, Inc.
95 Madison Avenue
New York, New York 10016

Visit us on the World Wide Web at http://www.dk.com

Library of Congress Cataloging-in-Publication Data
Willis, Jeanne.
The boy who lost his belly button / by Jeanne Willis; illustrated by Tony Ross.—1st American ed.
p.   cm.
"A DK Ink book."
Summary: When a young boy loses his belly button, he questions the jungle animals
and gets a surprise from the crocodile.
ISBN 0-7894-6164-1
[1. Belly button—Fiction. 2. Jungle animals—Fiction.] I. Ross, Tony, ill. II. Title.
PZ7.W68313 Bo 2000   [E]—dc21   99-055424

The text of this book is set in 18 point Garamond Infant.
Printed and bound in Italy.

First American Edition, 2000
2 4 6 8 10 9 7 5 3 1
Published in the United Kingdom by Andersen Press Ltd., London

Once there was a little boy who lost his belly button.

It was there when he went to sleep,
but when he woke up it was gone.
So he went into the jungle to look for it.

On the way, he met a giraffe.

"I've lost my belly button," explained the boy. "Do you know where it is?"
"Search me!" said the giraffe.
So the boy fetched a ladder and searched the giraffe.
He found a button, but it wasn't his.

"It's mine," said the giraffe.
"I've had it since the day I was born."

So the boy asked the gorilla.
"Have you found a belly button anywhere?"
"Yes," said the gorilla. "Right here."
And it stuck out its tummy.

"Very nice," said the boy, "but it's not mine."
"My mother gave it to me," said the gorilla.

Just then, the boy spotted a lion
sleeping on its back in the long grass.
He crept up and went through its fur
with a long-toothed comb.
The lion opened one eye.
"I was wondering if you'd borrowed
my belly button," said the boy politely.

"Why would I? I've got a perfectly good
one of my own," said the lion. "See?"

The boy saw.
"Have all animals got belly buttons?" he asked.
"Hands up, everyone who's got a belly button!"
roared the lion.

"Look, I've got a huge one,"
bellowed the elephant.

"I've got a teeny one," squeaked the mouse.

"I've got a warty one," grunted the warthog.

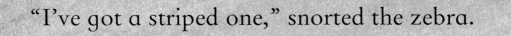

"I've got a striped one," snorted the zebra.

"And I've got a muddy one," gurgled the hippopotamus.

But the crocodile lay in the swamp as if it had
something to hide.
"How about crocodiles? Do they have belly buttons?"
"They might," sneered the crocodile.
"Show me!" cried the boy.
So the crocodile rolled over . . .

and right in the middle of its scaly, reptilian tummy
was something small and pink and round.
"What are you doing with my belly button?"
shouted the little boy.
"I'm washing the fluff out for you," said the crocodile.
"Thanks," said the boy. "Can I have it back now?"
"Certainly," smiled the crocodile. "Come and get it."

So the boy took off his clothes. . . .

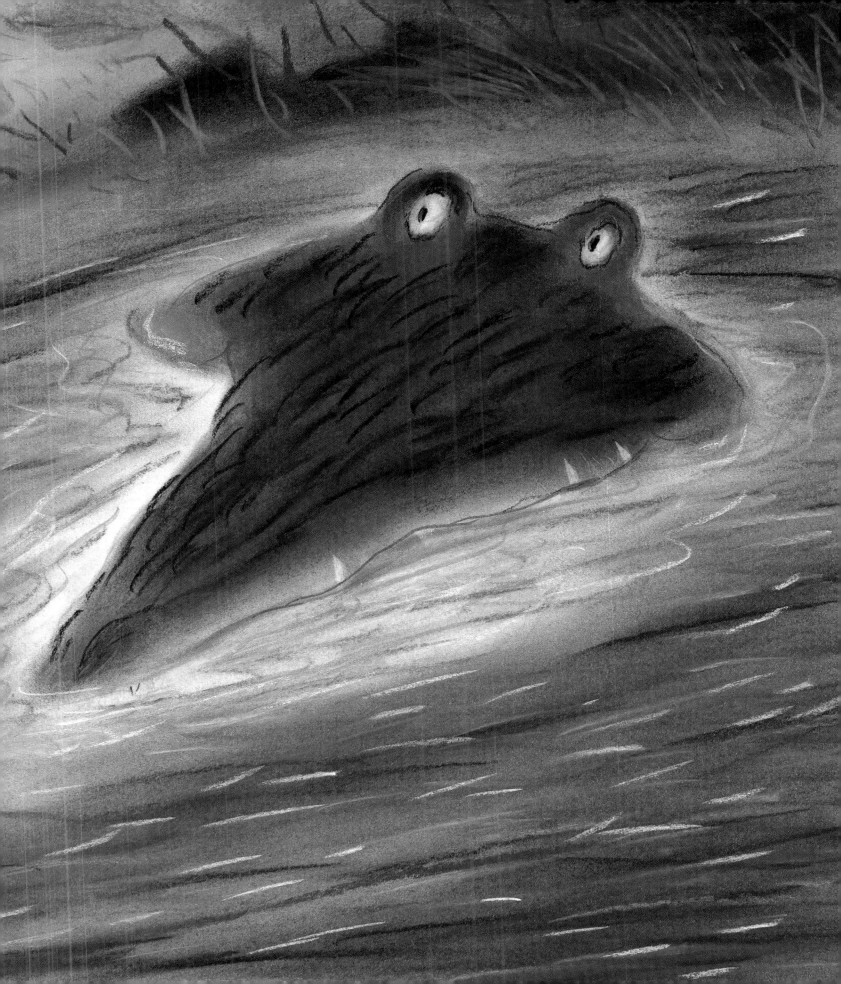

He waded right into the swamp.
And . . .

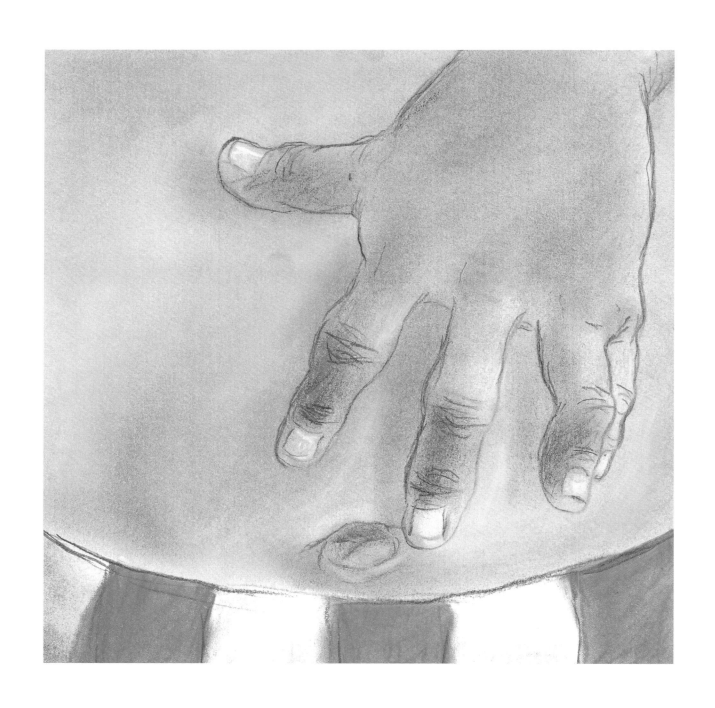

he GRABBED it!